Little Porcupine's Christmas

Little Porcupine's Christmas

By JOSEPH SLATE
Illustrated by FELICIA BOND

SCHOLASTIC INC.
New York Toronto London Auckland Sydney
Mexico City New Delhi Hong Kong Buenos Aires

ISBN 0-439-38038-3

Text copyright © 1982, 2001 by Joseph Slate.
Illustrations copyright © 1982 by Felicia Bond.
All rights reserved.
Published by Scholastic Inc., 555 Broadway, New York, NY 10012,
by arrangement with Laura Geringer Books, an imprint of HarperCollins Publishers.
SCHOLASTIC and associated logos are trademarks and/or
registered trademarks of Scholastic Inc.

12 11 10 9 8 7 6 5 4 3 2 1   1 2 3 4 5 6/0

Printed in Mexico   49

First Scholastic printing, November 2001

For the Godchildren—
Cassidy, Cathy, Jonathon, John,
Kevin, Kris, Mark, Marty,
Philip, Richard, Shannon, Steve,
Tim, and Wally

—J.S.

For Harriett Barton
—F.B.

It is time for the Christmas play.
Little Porcupine gives his mother
a big, ouchy hug.
"Oh Mama, I would so like a part," he says.
"Then you must try out," says Mama Porcupine.

Little Porcupine looks in his mirror.

He pops his spines. He crosses his eyes.

He stands on one foot.

"But I am too funny-looking," he says.

Mama gives Little Porcupine a big, prickly hug.

"You are not funny-looking," she says.

"Your spines shine. Your eyes sparkle. You are
the light of my life."

"The light of my life!"

Little Porcupine loves his mother's words.

He runs off to school.

There, the little animals are lined up for

parts in the Baby in the Manger play.

"My turn to try out," says Little Porcupine.

"No," says Fox. "You don't have red hair like me.
There is no part for you."

"You don't have stripes like me," says Chipmunk.

"And you don't have long ears like me," says Bunny.

"You are too funny-looking," says Cub Bear.

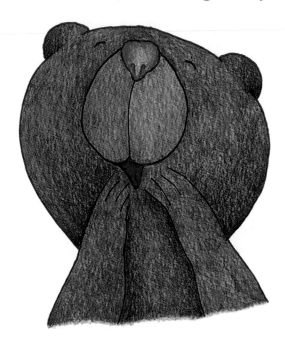

"You can be the stage crew," says Mouse.

"You can be the cleanup crew and pick up cotton snow with your spines," says Squirrel.

"And put the tinsel in the trash!" says Piggy.

"I could be a shepherd and carry the lamb,"
says Little Porcupine.

"Oh, no," says Lamb. "Not a shepherd. Your
spines would stick me."

"Or I could be a Wise Man and carry a gift."

"Oh, no, no," says Chick. "Not a Wise Man.

Your spines would punch the gift full of holes."

"I could be a king with a pointy crown."

"Oh no, no, no," says Raccoon.

"A stick ball like you cannot be a king."

"Stick Ball! Stick Ball!"

The little animals all laugh and hoot.

Little Porcupine runs home.

Tears roll down his spiny cheeks.

"I am just a stick ball,"
he says to his mother.
"Oh no," says Mama Porcupine.
"You are the light of my life."
And she gives him a
big, pinchy hug.

Four days before Christmas,
all the animals have a part.
All but Little Porcupine.

Three days before Christmas,

all the animals have a costume.

All but Little Porcupine.

Two days before Christmas,

all the animals know where to stand on stage.

All but Little Porcupine.

Now it is the night before Christmas,

the night of the Baby in the Manger play.

The mamas and papas are in their seats.

Little Porcupine peeks through the curtain.

He turns down the house lights.

He turns on the spotlights.

He pulls up the curtain.

Here is the Baby in the Manger.

"Ahhhhhhh," say the mamas.

"Ohhhhhhh," say the papas.

"But where is the star in the sky?" ask the mamas.
"Yes, where is the star the Wise Men follow to
the Baby in the Manger?" ask the papas.

"Oh dear! Oh, my! Oh, help!"
cry the animals. "We forgot the star."

Little Porcupine runs behind the manger. He climbs the big Christmas tree. He rolls up into a ball and lets his spines stick out.

"Little Porcupine is the star!" cry the animals.

"What a beautiful star," say the mamas and the papas.

"Star of my life!" says Mama Porcupine.

And way up high,

Little Porcupine lights up

all the others—a shiny, spiny star.